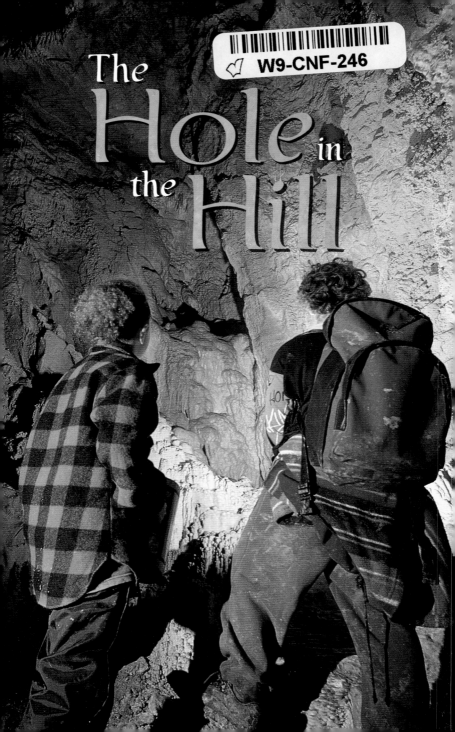

The
Hole in
the Hill

W9-CNF-246

CONTENTS

"It's true!" Leo shouted. "Mr. Williams, from the farm along the ridge, told me. Every few months, some of his livestock disappear without a trace."

The group of friends sat, talking around the campfire. Leo always told ridiculous

stories when they were camping. But this time, he sounded really serious.

"Then there was the time Joe McFinnis disappeared. Mr. Williams said Joe went off at dusk to check on the livestock. He never came back! The people who were in the search party still talk about the strange sounds they heard the night he disappeared."

"Yeah. I heard that story, too," Armandeep piped up.

"My dad was in the search party," Jimmy said. "He thinks there's something weird about that farm."

"What a load of garbage!" Holly scoffed. "Leo, you always try to scare us. Well, this year, it just hasn't worked. I guess we've outgrown your stupid scary stories."

"I'm telling you," Leo said, "there's something strange about the Williams's farm. I know, let's go exploring there tomorrow. Don't worry, we'll go in the daylight. I wouldn't want you to get scared or anything!"

The school holidays were always an opportunity for the group of friends to get together on Leo's family's farm. It had seemed to take years before their parents would allow them some "adult-free" time. But this year, they were allowed to light their own campfires, sleep in tents, and explore the acres of farm spread before them.

Their campsite was less than a fifteen-minute walk from the main farmhouse and bordered the boundary of the Williams's farm. For as long as Leo could remember, he had wanted to explore the neighboring property. Its stacks of pancake rocks and pockets of bush seemed to hide mysteries that Leo longed to uncover.

Early the next morning, an eerie mist covered the farm.

By the time Leo tossed a compass, flashlight, pocketknife, first-aid kit, and some sandwiches and drinks into a backpack, the mist had cleared.

"OK, who's coming?" Leo asked.

"I'm in," said Derek.

No one else spoke.

"Well, we're not hanging around waiting for you to make up your minds," said Derek. "Come on, Leo."

They walked only a short distance before the others caught up.

"Wait. We're coming, too," Holly said. "It's broad daylight, and your parents are just down the road. What could possibly go wrong?"

CHAPTER TWO

It wasn't long before the group were feeling the heat of the morning sun as they clambered up the hill littered with slabs of pancake rocks.

The rugged landscape was similar to the area near town where a large cave had been discovered.

Geologists who had come to study the cave had also visited the local school. They had explained that over millions of years, rainwater had trickled through the limestone rock, leaving chasms that reached far down into the earth.

As they poked their way into holes and gullies, the thought crossed Leo's mind that perhaps something similar lay beneath them now.

The group pushed their way through small pockets of bush, checking out every crack and ledge in the hill for signs of anything unusual.

"Only rabbits, weasels, and rocks!" Leo said. "What a waste of time."

"Did you really expect to find more?" Holly asked.

"No, I guess not. But a few old bones would have been good to spice up my scary stories," laughed Leo.

Suddenly, a strange rustling sound came from a clump of nearby bushes.

"What's that?" Leo asked.

"It must be the monster, *Whooooo!*" laughed Holly. "You'd better check it out, Leo," she challenged. "It might be the ghost of your missing man!"

"OK, I will," Leo replied, trying to sound more confident than he felt.

"Do you want to come with me, Derek? Just in case I need backup," Leo said with a shy grin.

The two boys eased their way through the clump of bushes. Ferns grazed their faces and twigs grabbed at their clothing.

Suddenly, there was a loud rumbling sound, and the earth began to shake violently. Leo grasped frantically at a fallen tree and just managed to grab ahold of a small branch as the ground opened beneath him.

Seconds seemed to stretch into hours as Leo hung over the dark gaping hole. Beads of sweat appeared on his forehead as he clung desperately to the flimsy branch.

"Help me, Derek!" he cried.

Stunned, Derek watched Leo's body swinging precariously over the deep hole. Then, suddenly coming to grips with the situation, he moved forward slowly and carefully.

"Just hang on, Leo. I'm coming. Holly, Armandeep, and Jimmy, you stay back. I think the ground is only stable enough for one of us.

"Leo, I'm going to crawl toward the edge. I'll tie one end of my scarf around this tree. When I get close enough, I'll throw you the other end. Grab it and I'll pull you up."

Carefully, he crawled forward, tied one end of the scarf around the tree, and stretched it out as far as he could. Derek could see his friend's frightened face. He had to reach Leo before he fell down into that hole!

CHAPTER THREE

Derek reached out further and swung the scarf within Leo's grasp. The weight of his body proved too much for the unstable ground. The earth crumbled beneath him and, before they knew what was happening, both of the boys were falling into the

dark chasm. Their screams echoed through the underground until they landed, with a sudden jolt, eighteen feet below the earth's surface.

The others watched in horror as their friends disappeared from sight. "Leo! Derek! Where are you?" they screamed.

But there was no reply. Without thinking, Jimmy rushed forward.

Holly pulled him back. "You can't go any closer," she said, "or you'll be next! Armandeep, you wait here. Jimmy, come with me. We need to get help."

Together, Holly and Jimmy ran as fast as they could across the farm.

Deep below the ground, a pile of mud and leaves had cushioned the boys' fall. They were dazed, frightened, and bruised. A sharp pain shot up Leo's arm, and he groaned loudly.

"Leo, are you OK?" Derek asked. In the darkness, he could just make out the shape of his best friend.

"My arm. I think it's broken."

"Can you move it?" Derek asked.

"A little. Maybe it's just sprained or something," Leo replied bravely.

The boys' eyes slowly adjusted to the darkness. They could see a comforting circle of light coming through the opening high above them.

They cupped their hands around their mouths and called out, "Help! Get us out of here."

Their voices echoed up the chasm. They waited. Then called again. There was no reply.

As she stared into the gaping hole, Armandeep could just make out a faint noise that sounded like talking.

"It's OK. I'm here, and the others have gone for help," she called back at the top of her voice.

But, underground, the terrified boys heard nothing.

Leo looked up and noticed dirt falling around them like a fine rain. "Move!" he yelled as he pushed Derek aside. A large slab of mud and branches plummeted down, landing just where they had been standing.

"It's not safe here," Leo said. "We have to move farther away from the opening before we get buried alive!"

Silently, Derek picked up his scarf from the pile of debris and followed Leo through a narrow passage, away from the comforting light of day.

"I'm scared. It's dark and cold and I want to get out," Derek whimpered.

Leo tried to comfort his friend, but he was having trouble fighting back tears of desperation.

As another stab of pain shot down his arm, Leo remembered the flashlight in the backpack. Gently, he eased the backpack over his sore arm and groped around until he found it. With a sigh of delight, he turned it on.

Leo cautiously flicked the beam around the passageway. Drops of water ran in tiny rivulets down the walls and formed a soft silty sludge on the cave floor. Carefully, the boys edged along the passage until they found a dry area beneath a small overhang.

"Turn the flashlight off, Leo. We need to save the batteries," Derek whispered.

It was black. Pitch black. The only sound was the soft plink of water droplets as they slid down the wall into small puddles on the floor below.

"Do you think the others will find us? What if no one comes?" Derek asked, his voice filled with fear.

"It'll be all right," Leo reassured him. "Someone will come soon."

The boys sat together in silence, each lost in his own thoughts.

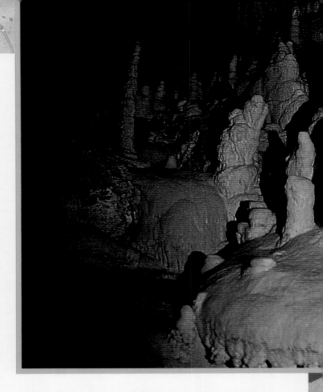

CHAPTER FOUR

An icy cold draught wafted through the cave, sending shivers up the boys' spines.

"We have to move. I can't stand just sitting here," Derek said. "Give me the flashlight, and we'll explore this passageway. Maybe there is a way out."

Leo hesitated. The ache in his arm was getting worse, and he could feel the muscles tightening up. He gave Derek the flashlight and, staying close to one another, the boys picked their way across the debris of fallen rocks.

As Derek swung the beam of light around the walls of the cave, a most amazing scene appeared before them.

Over millions of years, tiny deposits of calcium had gathered. Millimeter by millimeter, drip by drip, these deposits had grown, building the most elaborate set of formations.

The visiting geologists had talked about stalactites and stalagmites. The

boys were now surrounded by these great pillars of rock that hung from the ceiling like icicles, or strained upward from the floor of the cave. In places, the two grew tantalizingly close. In tens of thousands of years, they would link for eternity.

Leo and Derek gazed in awe.

"I don't like this. I think we should turn back. At least we could see a patch of daylight before," Derek said.

As they turned to pick their way back down the slope, the flashlight flickered. The boys shone the flashlight down toward the passageway. But the rocks and shadows seemed to taunt and tease them, creating illusions of passageways everywhere.

"There it is!" Derek called, moving toward a dark opening.

"No, it's over this way," Leo insisted. "I recognize that big stalactite hanging near it."

"But this one has a stalactite, too!" Derek insisted.

It was no use. By now, the boys were totally lost, and panic began to set in.

CHAPTER FIVE

"Look, we've got to calm ourselves down," Leo said reassuringly. "Why don't we have some lunch? Maybe then we'll feel better. Pass the flashlight. I'll see what I have in the backpack."

Leo knew that how they reacted over the next few

hours was crucial to their survival. He must start to think clearly. He pulled out their lunches from the bottom of the pack. The boys knew this food could be their last for a while, so they rationed it into small portions.

They huddled together, nibbling slowly on the sandwiches and fruit. As they turned off the flashlight to save the batteries, the black cloak of darkness wrapped itself around them. The two boys lay down on the cold cave floor and tried to get some rest.

The aching pain in Leo's arm woke him up. As he changed positions, he thought he saw movement in the darkness. Nudging Derek awake, Leo whispered, "Can you see something?"

"No. I don't think so," Derek replied.

"Give me the flashlight," Leo said urgently. "There is something there."

Leo grabbed the flashlight and swung the beam of light around the room. Shadows and shapes raced across the limestone walls. As the light reached the far end of the cavern, two dark shapes slipped out of view.

"It's the rescuers!" exclaimed Derek. "They didn't see us!"

35

Panicking, the boys grabbed the backpack and raced after the shadows. Their flashlight beam created great arcs on the walls and sent shapes racing around them. Leo and Derek called out loudly as they ran, their voices echoing in the empty cave. But the shadows kept moving, disappearing into the darkness ahead. Exhausted and confused, the boys collapsed onto the cold cave floor.

Leo rubbed his gritty eyes and watched as, once again, the shadows seemed to take on human form. The broad shapes of two men loomed from the darkness. They wore boots and rough old-fashioned clothing, and they appeared to be carrying lanterns.

The boys stared, unbelieving, as the strange shapes began to move silently around the cavern. Again, Leo called out to the shadowy figures. There was no reply.

"Wave the flashlight at them, maybe they're deaf," suggested Derek.

Frantically, Leo waved his flashlight. The beam was getting weaker by the minute. The figures flickered and raced around the giant cavern, then they disappeared from sight.

"Come on, we have to follow them," Leo shouted in the darkness.

"There is nothing to follow, Leo. Nothing!" screamed Derek. "Don't you understand? It's just your flashlight beam creating shadows. You're seeing what you want to. Nothing else!"

Defeated, Leo finally gave in. He let the tears come. The pain in his arm was excruciating, and he cradled it close to his body.

Remembering the first-aid kit in the backpack, Derek quickly found a reel of narrow white bandage. He felt grateful for the first-aid classes they'd had at school as he wound the bandage around Leo's hand and wrist and then secured a sling behind his neck. He found a mild painkiller in the kit and, holding the water bottle to Leo's lips, encouraged him to swallow it.

"It'll be OK, Leo," he said. "I'm sure the others went for help. A rescue team is probably on their way now. We're going to get out of here."

CHAPTER SIX

Far above the confusing labyrinth of underground tunnels, Holly and Jimmy had returned with help. Leo's mother, a team of experienced cavers, and James Williams had joined Armandeep beside the opening in the ground.

Carefully, the cavers examined the area. Loose rocks and unstable soil made them fear a further avalanche. There had to be another, safer entrance to the cave.

Then Denise, one of the cavers, said, "I remember hearing about an underground chamber discovered a hundred or so years ago by miners searching for minerals. Apparently, there is a steep shaft that leads into it somewhere near a high pyramid of stacked limestone rocks."

"I think I know the place!" James Williams exclaimed. He set off across the field. The others followed closely behind him.

Underground, the pain in Leo's arm had become unbearable. His body was slowly shutting down. He was drowsy and no longer felt like talking.

Derek tried to keep Leo warm and comfortable. He didn't know what to do other than lay down next to his best friend and listen to his shallow breathing. The flashlight gave one last flicker of light, then died. Once more, it was pitch black and deathly quiet.

Soon Derek, too, began to drift into a troubled sleep. In his dreams, he could hear echoing voices and the clinking of metal. Lights began to flicker on and off. He stirred. Sensing a presence, Derek woke up. He could hear noises! Real noises!

Looking up, Derek saw Denise rappelling, slowly but surely, down a narrow shaft only fifteen feet away. As Denise dropped to the floor of the cave, Derek burst into tears of relief. Silently, he pointed to the sleeping Leo.

After checking out Leo's injuries, Denise carefully fitted him with a rappelling harness and clipped it to the surface line. She took his good arm and wrapped it securely around the rope.

"Now, just hold on," Denise said. "It's all over. It's going to be all right." She took a small walkie-talkie from her backpack. "Up rope," she instructed.

Gently, Leo began to rise up the chimney. Derek followed soon after.

As they emerged from the shaft, the sun was just setting. Daylight was over and, once more, darkness was creeping in. But this time, it was a darkness both boys were happy to greet.

Do you like places that are deep, dark, and scary? We don't. However, when our caving friend Nick Andreef from Waitomo Adventures invited us to visit his underground world, we couldn't refuse.

Nick lead us through narrow winding tunnels until we emerged into a huge chamber. Stalactites and stalagmites were all around us. The sight was breathtaking.

We started to wonder what would happen if some children fell through a hole in a hill and ended up lost underground. The idea for this story was planted.

Taking photographs for *The Hole in the Hill* was very difficult. First, we had to find five children who would not be afraid to come caving with us. They had to be very patient; caving photography takes a long time.

There were lots of problems: Andy needed to keep his expensive equipment clean, his warm breath caused his viewfinder to fog up, water kept dripping off the roof onto the camera, and he could only see with the help of a flashlight and his helmet light.

Shooting images for *The Hole in the Hill* was cold, wet, dark, dirty work... but it was also lots of fun.

Angie and Andy Belcher

Challenges and Choices
Call of the Selkie
Trailblazers!
The Hole in the Hill
The Good, the Bad,
and Everything Else
On the Edge
The Willow Pattern

Our Wild World
Isn't It Cool? Discovering Antarctica
and the Arctic
The Horse, of Course
Trapped by a Teacher
Mystery Bay
The Rain Forest
Feathery Fables

That's a Laugh
Queen of the Bean
Cinderfella's Big Night
The Flying Pig and the Daredevil Dog
Ants Aren't Antisocial
Charlotte's Web Page
Playing with Words

Thrills and Spills
Mountain Bike Mania
Destination Disaster
Journey to the New World
The Secret of Bunratty Castle
Happy Accidents!
The Chocolate Flier

Written by **Angie Belcher**
Photographed by **Andy Belcher**
Edited by **Frances Bacon**
Designed by **Kristie Rogers**
The author and photographer would like to thank Waitomo Adventures.

04 03 02 01 00
10 9 8 7 6 5 4 3 2

Distributed in the United States by
RIGBY
a division of Reed Elsevier Inc.
P.O. Box 797
Crystal Lake, IL 60039-0797

Printed in Hong Kong.
ISBN: 0-7699-0414-9